The Lion Tamer
and the Lion

The Bears

The Band

The Horses

Story based on the Walt Disney motion picture *DUMBO* suggested by the story *Dumbo, the Flying Elephant* by Helen Aberson and Harold Perl. Copyright 1939 by Rollabook Publishers, Inc.

Published by Scholastic Inc., 90 Old Sherman Turnpike, Danbury, Connecticut 06816.

For information regarding permission, write to:
Disney Licensed Publishing, 114 Fifth Avenue, New York, New York 10011.

ISBN 0-7172-6057-7

Printed in the U.S.A. First printing, November 2003

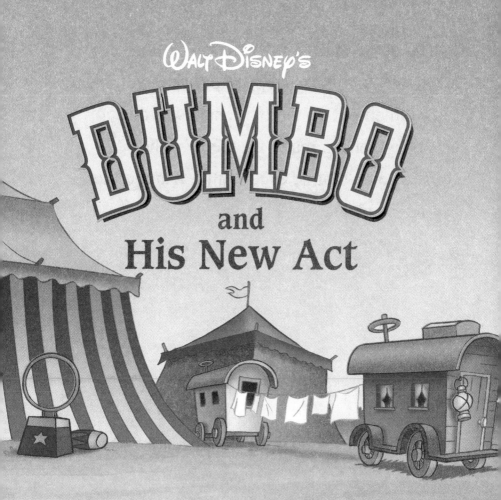

Walt Disney's DUMBO
and
His New Act

SCHOLASTIC INC.

New York   Toronto   London   Auckland   Sydney
Mexico City   New Delhi   Hong Kong   Buenos Aires

The circus was in town! Camels, horses, elephants, and bears stepped out of the circus train. Strong men put up the big tent. Everyone was busy getting ready for the first show.

Everyone, that is, except little Dumbo the Flying Elephant.

"Hey, Dumbo, why so glum?" said Timothy
Mouse to his friend.

"Oh, I know," said Timothy. "You're tired of performing the same old Dumbo the Flying Elephant act, aren't you? I suppose you want to try something new— something more exciting."

Dumbo nodded his head.

Dumbo and Timothy stepped into the big tent. They saw the magnificent white horses rehearsing their act. Dumbo loved watching the horses prance around the ring in their fancy headdresses and saddles.

"I think you'd be good at this," said Timothy to Dumbo. "You can be Dumbo the Elegant Elephant."

"Perfect!" remarked Timothy, as he fastened a feathered headdress onto Dumbo. Then Timothy put a fancy saddle on Dumbo.

"Now just keep your head up," instructed Timothy. "You'll be the world's most elegant elephant."

DUMBO

THE ELEGANT ELEPHANT

Dumbo stepped into the ring with the horses.

The monkeys giggled. They thought he looked silly.

Dumbo didn't pay any attention to the monkeys though. He just tried his best to prance along in a graceful way.

But then Dumbo tripped over his ears. He stumbled and fell. Timothy rushed over.

"Don't worry, Dumbo," said Timothy. "We'll find a new act that's more your style."

Dumbo and Timothy walked over to where the lion tamer and the lion were rehearsing their act.

"Hey! How about Dumbo the Fearless Elephant?" Timothy asked Dumbo. "I like the sound of that!"

"Come on, Dumbo. Let's try it," said Timothy. "Of course, we won't use fire until we're good at it," he added.

As usual, the monkeys tried to get into the act. They turned up dressed in firefighter costumes and carrying a hose. Dumbo and Timothy ignored the silly monkeys.

"Now start running and
jump straight through the hoop,"
coached Timothy.

Dumbo ran and jumped just as he was
instructed. But his ears didn't fit through the hoop.

"Oh, dear!" Timothy exclaimed. "It's a good
thing we didn't light the fire!"

As soon as the monkeys heard
the word *fire*, they rushed over to
Dumbo and sprayed him with
water from the hose.

Timothy dried his sad,
wet friend. "Don't worry,
Dumbo," he comforted,
"keep trying. We'll find
a new act that's more
your style."

The two friends went back into the big tent. The trapeze artists were rehearsing their act. Dumbo and Timothy watched the performers swing from trapeze to trapeze with the greatest of ease.

"Now this is an act where your ears won't get in the way!" said Timothy excitedly. "Dumbo the Acrobatic Elephant has a nice ring to it—don't you think?"

DUMBO

THE ACROBATIC
ELEPHANT

Dumbo and Timothy waited
for the performers to finish. Then
Dumbo flew to the platform and
grabbed a trapeze.

"One, two, three—
GO!" shouted Timothy
from the opposite
platform.

Dumbo held onto the
trapeze and swung through
the air. After a few seconds,
Timothy pushed another
trapeze towards him.

The little elephant grabbed the second
trapeze with his trunk, causing him to stop
in midair. Dumbo was stuck!

"Just let go of one trapeze!"
shouted Timothy.

Dumbo held tight and seemed confused.
The monkeys watched and chattered from the
net below.

"Let go!" shouted Timothy.

Suddenly—much to Timothy's alarm—
Dumbo let go of both trapezes
at the same time!

Dumbo fell towards
the net below.

When Dumbo landed in the net, it sank way, way down. Then—*WHOOSH!* The net sprang way, way up! Dumbo sailed towards the top of the tent. The monkeys bounced and shrieked with laughter.

Just when Dumbo reached
the top of the tent, his ears
filled with air. He began to fly!
"Way to go, Dumbo!"
called a much-relieved Timothy.
The monkeys cheered.

Back on the ground, Timothy tried to cheer up Dumbo.

"Don't worry, Dumbo," reassured Timothy. "We'll find a new act that's more your style."

"We'll just keep trying," promised Timothy. "You never know when the next great idea is going to come along."

Dumbo smiled happily. Just then the bear family entered the ring.

The baby was learning
a new act, too. He was
trying to roll a barrel while
balancing on it.

It wasn't easy . . .

. . . but at last he succeeded!

Then Timothy and Dumbo watched as the entire
bear family rehearsed their act. The bears balanced
and juggled, while riding their unicycles.

Timothy stroked his chin thoughtfully. "What
do you think about trying this act? You can be
Dumbo the Balancing Elephant!"

So Dumbo tried it. At
first, he was a little wobbly.
But then, with patience and
the advice of his friend,
Dumbo gained his balance
and began to pedal.

"Way to go,
Dumbo!" cheered
Timothy.

Dumbo rode proudly across the ring. But
Dumbo forgot to watch where he was going. And
he didn't know how to stop!

"Dumbo! Look out!" shouted Timothy.

But it was too late! *BANG!* The unicycle
hit the side of the ring.

Dumbo was thrown off. He sailed through the
air and landed in the snack bar with a *CRASH!*

Poor Dumbo wasn't hurt, but he *was* a mess! The monkeys thought Dumbo looked extremely funny.

"Oh, dear," fussed Timothy, trying to wipe off the mess. "You need a good bath. Come on. It's almost show time."

Dumbo soaked while
Timothy scrubbed his
back. They could hear
the audience arriving.
Excited children's
voices filled the night air.

From the tub, Dumbo and Timothy could see
the band warming up. As usual, the monkeys were
fooling around. One put a banana into the tuba.
When the tuba player blew a note, the banana flew
out and was caught by another monkey.

Dumbo and Timothy
laughed and laughed.
Then Dumbo had an idea.

When the band left
to change into their
uniforms, Dumbo
filled his trunk with
soapy water.

Then he poured
the soapy water
into the band's
instruments.

Soon after, the band returned. They picked up their instruments and began to march into the circus ring.

"Time to put on your costume, Dumbo," Timothy said. "Your act is first—right after the band plays the opening number."

Dumbo and Timothy
watched the band begin to
play. With every note,
bubbles poured out of the
instruments. The audience
loved it!

Then Dumbo filled his trunk
with soapy water once again.

"Great idea!"
exclaimed Timothy
when he realized
what his friend was
up to. With that,
Dumbo flew into
the circus ring.

The audience cheered
wildly as Dumbo soared out
over them. He blew bubbles
until the circus tent was filled
with them. The children were
especially delighted. They
clapped and waved and tried
to catch the bubbles.

"Wow!" said Timothy when
Dumbo's performance was over.
"You're Dumbo the Flying
Elephant—with Bubbles!
I think we've found a new act
that's just your style!"